The **Principal's**
Night Before Christmas

The Principal's
Night Before Christmas

By Steven L. Layne
Illustrated by James Rice

PELICAN PUBLISHING COMPANY
Gretna 2004

For Dr. Debbie LeBlanc, who leads with integrity and
never loses sight of what it's really all about

The word "Pelican" and the depiction of a pelican are trademarks
of Pelican Publishing Company, Inc., and are registered in the
U.S. Patent and Trademark Office.

Library of Congress-in-Publication Data

Layne, Steven L.
    The principal's night before Christmas / by Steven L. Layne ; illustrated by James Rice.
        p. cm.
    ISBN 1-58980-252-7 (alk. paper)
    1. School principals—Juvenile poetry. 2. Santa Claus—Juvenile poetry.
3. Christmas—Juvenile poetry. 4. Children's poetry, American. I. Rice, James. II. Title.

PS3612.A96P75 2004
813'.54—dc22

                                    2004008657

Printed in Singapore
Published by Pelican Publishing Company, Inc.
1000 Burmaster Street, Gretna, Louisiana 70053

THE PRINCIPAL'S NIGHT
BEFORE CHRISTMAS

'Twas the night before Christmas
And all through the town
All the students and teachers
Had settled right down.

The school parties and pageants
Had ended their run
And the stress was all gone
Now that break had begun.

But poor Principal Swell
Still had so much to do
That when Christmas Eve came
He was in quite a stew.

There were forms to fill out
For state-mandated testing
Plus some standardized ovals
To darken—no jesting!

And he'd promised to fix
Miss Schmidt's PC work station

While custodian Carl
Was in Guam on vacation.

Then the bus routes were giving
Him headaches galore
For the school board had told him
He'd better explore

A *much* faster trip
To the Vandertrapp home,
Where dear Rachel's sweet mama
Stood right by the phone

To report that the bus
Had once more arrived late
(And the stress this caused Rachel
One dared not debate).

And another bus driver
Had threatened she'd quit
Because Peter McDermott
Continued to spit

And to scream and to pout
And to bully small kids
And to make some girls faint
When he flipped his eyelids.

But young Peter's parents
Had threatened they'd sue
When the driver had chastised
Their boy, for they knew

He was truly an angel—
They'd said it before—
In at least sixteen meetings
In grades three and four.

Mr. Swell had to map out
A plan over break
That would bring resolution
For everyone's sake.

And he'd promised to work out
Some field-trip details
So the third graders' trip
To see mantas and whales

At the zoo's new exhibit
Would continue as planned,
Even though he'd been told
That *all* field trips were banned

By the superintendent,
Dr. Donald S. Late,
Who'd proclaimed, just last week,
That the risks were too great!

So after his own kids
Were tucked in at eight
The good principal raced off
To school to create

Just as many solutions
As could ever be mustered.
Oh, he sat deep in thought
But soon found himself flustered

By the jingle of bells,
The alarm losing power,
And a jolly voice questioning,
"*School* at this hour?"

"I just sent the teachers
All home from the mall
And it seems I'm now paying
Their bosses a call."

"Well, I have a few words
That I want you to hear.
Your devotion to children
And teachers brings cheer

To the big heart of Santa,
Who knows what is true.
And this school district's lucky
It's held on to you."

"Now, I've seen the McDermotts;
I've checked out the zoo;
And I made the elves darken
Those ovals for you!"

"All the rest will be managed,
Completed, or fixed.
It's a promise to count on—
It's one of St. Nick's."

"Go on home now, my friend,"
Santa said with a wink,
And before Mr. Swell
Even knew what to think

That lively professor
Had boarded his bus
And it took to the air
Without making much fuss.

His eyes were a-twinkling
As the bus flew on past.
But his voice rang with strength
As he shouted at last—

"Merry Christmas to principals—
Holiday cheer!
For they make Santa proud
Every day of the year!"